MARGRET & H. A. REY'S

Curious George
at the Aquarium

by R. P. Anderson

Illustrated in the style of H. A. Rey by Anna Grossnickle Hines

HOUGHTON MIFFLIN HARCOURT

Boston New York

www.hmhco.com

The text of this book is set in Adobe Garamond.
The illustrations are watercolor.

Library of Congress Cataloging-in-Publication Data
Anderson, R. P. (Robert Pierce), 1969–
Margret & H. A. Rey's Curious George at the aquarium / by R. P. Anderson ;
illustrated in the style of H. A. Rey by Anna Grossnickle Hines.
p. cm.
Margret and H. A. Rey's Curious George at the aquarium
Summary: When George and the man with the yellow hat visit the aquarium, George's
curiosity gets the better of him and he accidentally joins some of the exhibits.

ISBN: 978-0-544-17674-4

[1. Monkeys—Fiction. 2. Aquariums, Public—Fiction. 3. Marine animals—Fiction.]
I. Rey, Margret. II. Rey, H. A. (Hans Augusto), 1898–1977. III. Hines,
Anna Grossnickle, ill. IV. Title. V. Title: Margret and H. A. Rey's Curious George
at the aquarium. VI. Title: Curious George at the aquarium.
PZ7.A54888Mar 2007   [E]—dc22   2006031367

Manufactured in China
SCP 10 9 8 7 6 5 4 3 2

4500517450

This is George.

He was a good little monkey and always very curious.

Today George and the man with the yellow hat were visiting the aquarium.

"George," said the man, "please wait here while I buy the tickets."

George tried to wait, but he was so excited! What was inside?

He wanted to look over the walls, but they were too high.

Just then, he heard a *SPLASH!*
and a *WHOOSH!* Water flew high
into the air. People cheered. What
could that be? George was curious.

He hopped over the gate into the aquarium. How surprised he was!

Swimming right in front of George were two beluga whales!
The mother and baby beluga whale swam right past him.

And not far away was a family of sea lions, diving and splashing. What fun!

George noticed people walking toward a big door—could there be more to see? He followed the crowd.

Now where was he? It was darker
inside and there were fish everywhere!
George did not know where to look first.

In one tank there were sharp-toothed piranhas,

in another tank there were seahorses,

and in another tank there was a large red octopus!

George saw a group of children across the room. An aquarium staff member was pointing to different sea creatures. "This is a starfish, this is a clam, and this is an urchin."

Nearby, there was a long, low, colorful tank. It was perfect for touching!

George was curious. As he reached his hand into the water, a large crab came scuttling out from under a rock and right toward his finger!

Snap!

Ouch!

Poor George. He did not like this exhibit.

DO NOT TOUCH

George slipped out a door into the sunlight. But, oh! What was going on here?

George saw fat, funny-looking black and white fish flying under the water. As he watched they flew up out of the water. "What kind of fish does that, and where did they go?" George wondered.

George climbed up and into their exhibit.

They were not fish at all, but penguins, of course!

George hopped like a penguin,

flapped his wings like a penguin,

and waddled like a penguin.

A crowd gathered and laughed.
But when he slid on his belly like a penguin . . .

The aquarium staff stopped by to check on the penguins.

"A monkey! In the penguin exhibit?"

George opened a door to escape, but instead . . . all the penguins ran out! Penguins, penguins everywhere!

The staff was angry at George. How could they catch all the penguins?

In all the excitement nobody noticed the penguin chick falling into the water! No one but George.

The baby penguin hadn't learned to swim yet. As only a monkey can, George scaled the rope hanging over the beluga tank and swung over the water, saving the chick.

The director of the aquarium and the man with the yellow hat heard the commotion and came running.

"That monkey helped the baby penguin," said a boy in the crowd.
"No one else could have saved him," said a girl.
The director thanked George for his help and made him an
honorary staff member of the aquarium.

George said goodbye to his new penguin friends. He could not wait to come back to the aquarium and visit them again!